Yanni Rubbish

Yanni Rubbish

by Shulamith Levey Oppenheim
Illustrated by Doug Chayka

Boyd Mills Press

Text copyright © 1999 by Shulamith Levey Oppenheim
Illustrations copyright © 1999 by Doug Chayka

Published by Caroline House
Boyds Mills Press, Inc.
A Highlights Company
815 Church Street
Honesdale, Pennsylvania 18431
Printed in China

Publisher Cataloging-in-Publication Data
Oppenheim, Shulamith Levey
Yanni rubbish / by Shulamith Levey Oppenheim : illustrated by
Doug Chayka.—1st edition.
[32]p. : col. ill. ; cm.
Summary: A young boy is taunted by friends because of his job
collecting garbage in a small Greek village.
ISBN 1-56397-668-4
1. Greece—Juvenile fiction. [1. Greece—Fiction.] I. Chayka, Doug,
ill. II. Title.
[E]—dc21 1999 AC CIP
Library of Congress Catalog Card No. 98-71791

First edition, 1999
The text of this book is set in 14-point Palatino.
The illustrations are done in oil.

10 9 8 7 6 5 4 3 2 1

For Ann and Rick, with love
—S. L. O.

To Skylar
—D. C.

Yanni came out of the house pulling on his cotton trousers, his dark hair falling over sleepy eyes. His mother had left early to work in the village bakery. His father was in Germany helping to build skyscrapers for very rich people.

"*Kalimera*, Lamia, good morning," he called to the small gray donkey trotting up to greet him. Yanni dropped a bucket into the well by the corner of a stone wall. He splashed some of the cold sweet water on his face and chest. Then he poured the rest into Lamia's wooden drinking trough. Jumping over the fence, he returned with an armload of flowering clover and spread it before her.

Yanni patted Lamia's nose. "I love the early morning. If only I didn't have to spend the day collecting trash. But Papa said I should try to take his place, so that when he returns we'll still have the business. He said there's not much work for a stonemason in the village.

"But . . ." he continued softly. Lamia was munching loudly on the clover. "But all those bags full of smelly bottles and rags and pieces of tires and metal that cuts my hands and the worst part . . . ." Tears welled up in Yanni's eyes.

"I keep the streets clean and they—Oh, let's go." He ran the back of his hand across his eyes. "We have to do it, Lamia, for Papa and Mama. I'll be right back."

And Yanni went inside to his breakfast of tea with thick bread and honey.

After he had hitched Lamia to the wagon, Yanni climbed up onto the seat. It was loose at one end. The piece of old rug his mother had given him kept slipping and the rough wood hurt his thighs. As he came down the narrow street into the village, his stomach tightened. There they were, his friends, playing marbles beside the road. Cleanthi and Yorgos and Alexi. He went to school with them, he swam with them, he even went to church with them. And . . . as the wagon rumbled past the three boys, he heard them call out, as they did every time they saw him come through to collect the trash. "Ho, ho, your donkey's lame and Yanni Rubbish is your name!" They didn't even look up.

"Don't stop, Lamia," Yanni whispered to the donkey. "We have to keep the business going. They think it's a joke. But I'll have to think of something to stop them."

The morning grew hotter than usual and the trash in front of each house and store was mountain high. Yanni and Lamia were on their second trip, trudging up the narrow cart-path to the plateau behind a stand of pine and cypress. Lamia waited patiently, flicking off the flies that massed around her while Yanni tossed the trash onto the dump site. When he was finished, Yanni gave a gentle pat to Lamia's flank. The wagon was empty but the path was rutted and stony and the wagon needed new wheels.

That evening Yanni and his mother sat under their olive tree. The sea below edged the rocks with crystal-clear aqua. Further out the water was blue-black. Tiny whitecaps bobbed like gulls floating on the waves.

Lamia dozed beside mother and son. She was never hobbled or tethered. "If an animal is treated kindly, with respect and love, it gives back love," Yanni's father had told him. Now, watching Lamia doze, Yanni remembered his father's words. So what was the matter with his friends? Their parents loved them, he was sure. He had to find a way of stopping them from yelling out that foolish rhyme. He had to try.

"Mama," Yanni was sitting cross-legged in front of her. "I miss Papa so much."

His mother put down her knitting and stroked his cheek. "So do I, *krysomou*, my treasure. But we must be patient. Papa wants to send us enough money to build a second floor on our house and buy some lovely furniture. Then he will come home." Suddenly she jumped up. Her face was all smiles. "Just a minute," she said, and ran into the house. A few moments later she was back with a large envelope.

"I just remembered that I had this picture. I've wanted to frame it all these years." And she handed Yanni an old photograph. There were his parents sitting together on the seat of a beautiful wagon, looking so happy.

"Mama, you look just like Aunt Elena, and she's only fifteen."

"This was our wedding day," Yanni's mother announced proudly. "And I wasn't much older than my sister is now. I'm glad I found the picture. We'll keep it on the dresser. It will be as if Papa were with us."

Yanni stared at the photo. "Mama, is that Lamia pulling the wagon?"

"Heavens, no. That's Gigi, Lamia's mother. This was taken nine years ago, almost a year before you were born."

"Mama, what is Gigi wearing?" Yanni pointed to the donkey's neck.

"That?" His mother peered closely. "Why, that's a necklace of braided ribbon I made. I must have it somewhere!" Once again she rushed into the house. Yanni kept looking at the picture. The wagon didn't have a board out of place. All the wheels had spokes. It was a beautiful wagon. If only . . .

His thoughts were interrupted by a clear tinkling sound. He looked up. There was his mother holding out a broad circlet of yellow, green, and red braided ribbons, with three large blue beads and a bell.

Yanni ran to his mother. He had an idea. "Mama, you know how my friends tease me about collecting rubbish—"

She pulled him close to her. "I know, dearest Yanni, and how I wish I could do something about it."

"There is, Mama, there is something we can do. We can fix up the wagon. It doesn't have to look like it's falling apart just because it's a rubbish wagon. We can paint it and put a new seat in front and Lamia can wear that beautiful necklace. I'll bet my friends will be surprised. They might even ask me for a ride." Yanni's eyes sparkled.

"Mama, can we take a few drachmas from our savings? I know Papa would say, 'It's a fine idea, Yanni, and you thought of it yourself!' " Yanni looked at his mother. He saw that her cheeks were wet.

"I think we can," she answered softly. "I'm sure we can."

So Yanni's mother asked their neighbor Tonio to make new wheels and a new seat. Yanni and his mother painted the wagon a bright, bright blue because that was the color when it was new. Yanni had the idea to paint "Stavros and Son" on one side.

The very next time Yanni came down his narrow street into the village, his friends were kneeling beside the road playing with marbles. A clear tinkling sound made them look up. Lamia was wearing the necklace. Yanni's mother had brushed every bit of dust from the donkey's sturdy little body and trimmed her mane. Yanni was sitting on the new wide padded seat wearing a very starched white shirt.

Not one boy spoke. They just stared and stared as Yanni got down and began tossing the bags of trash into the wagon.

Then, the next time he appeared, coming back from the dump, they were waiting for him at the bottom of the cart-path.

"That's a fine wagon, Yanni." Alexi blushed and kicked a stone across the road.

"Lamia is really a good-looking donkey." There were two bright red spots on Cleanthi's cheeks.

"Yanni, how about a ride?" Yorgos stretched out his hand to his friend. "*Parakalo*, please?"

"Certainly," Yanni answered. "Climb in. There's still another load to collect!"